Raw Mangoes

A Collection of Short Stories

Supriya Barsode

NOTION PRESS

NOTION PRESS

India. Singapore. Malaysia.

ISBN xxx-x-xxxxx-xx-x

About the Author

Supriya Barsode was introduced to literature in her school years and has always believed in the magic of words. She studied to be a doctor and practices to date; this magic has held on.

She has published a book of poems, 'Rhyme nor Reason', and two awesome adventure mysteries for children, 'The Underground Mystery', and 'The Lakeside Mystery'.

This is a collection of short stories about people from different walks of life, their struggles and triumphs.

Dedication

This book is dedicated to my grandmother Sudha, who regaled me with many tales in my childhood, and my mother Sadhana, whose level-headed advice helped me keep my feet firmly on the ground.

Contents

Preface vi

1. Clipped Nails 1

2. Hasinabi 7

3. The Outhouse 15

4. Conference 22

5. Shani Neecham 27

6. Autumn Leaves 33

7. Raw Mangoes 38

8. Yellappa 47

9. Dirty Linen 53

10. Full Circle 60

11. An Indian Summer 68

12. An Exchange 73

13. Scorpion 86

Preface

A collection of short stories that takes you on a compelling journey from a village to a city, from a beach to a hut.

As Hasinabi follows her love, only to have her past catch up with her. Savitri is enjoying her sister's wedding preparations and learning what growing up is the hard way. Rani's special bond with her grandparents and a look at death through the eyes of a child. The visit to the old home where a yard full of autumn leaves touches one's heart, and the antics of an exchange student, and so many more stories that will tug at your heart or leave you mulling over, and some might even bring a smile.

"Inside each of us is a natural-born storyteller, waiting to be released."

— Robin Moore, author

Author name: Supriya Barsode

1. Clipped Nails

Running out to the iron gate, I stood next to Granny, peering out through the floral designs on the wrought iron gates.

"Aah! There he comes," murmured 'Aaji'(my grandmother), making sure that her sari pleats were in place as we watched 'Ajoba' (my grandfather) pedal slowly towards us, the rickety bicycle, sending out all sorts of noises, announcing his arrival to one and all.

Ajji had married Ajoba at the very young age of fourteen. He was ten years older than her and her elder brother's best friend. It was a love marriage turned into an arranged one. Aunt Shubra used to always tease her about it. At six feet, Ajoba must have been irresistible to my petite Ajji. Now, his balding head perched atop broad shoulders was his most distinguishing feature. Ajoba came from a small, obscure village near the western part of India, caked in Nandwad. One of twenty children, his childhood was a long list of wants. His stepmother was dead against spending any money on his education. One day, sick of her relentless taunting, Ajoba burnt his college books in the courtyard and got himself enlisted in the army.

Retirement wasn't easy for him as his pension barely covered the monthly expenses. Living in two rented rooms with a daughter yet to be married and another widowed, and staying with them with her five-year-old daughter was very difficult indeed. His life was one long string of jobs and overtime to earn some extra money for his daughter's marriage. At present, he was a supervisor in a factory and cycled twenty kilometers to work. He also did some odd jobs around the factory owner's bungalow. With no education to speak of and in his late fifties, he had accepted his life.

"Hi! Ajoba," I jumped up and down wildly as he drew near us. He was so tired and could barely manage a smile. Sweat was trickling down his forehead, and his lips were pursed and turning an unhealthy blue. He swore he'd never touch them now, but I had seen him smoking sometimes behind the house.

"You must be tired," said Ajji, taking his cloth bag, and Ajoba managed one nod and a 'hmm', and we all set back walking to the house.

My mother was a receptionist at a clinic nearby and got a modest amount every month. Aunt was in her last year of college, already looking for a job. Every little bit helped.

"Kasa ahes beta?"(How are you, child?) Ajoba asked me, patting my head while he eased himself into the 'Aram Kursi'(Easy Chair) with a visible sigh.

It was his favourite chair, which was always kept outside, under the neem tree, except of course when it rained.

Ajoba often sat here reading the newspaper, having his daily cup of tea.

"Ajoba!"

"Yes, Beta," Ajoba answered absently, bending down to remove the metal clip trouser fasteners.

"Where do people go when they die?"

"Why are you asking this question?" Ajoba asked me with a concerned look on his face.

"My school friend Radha's uncle died yesterday, and she told me he was never coming back."

"People go to God's house when they die because he loves them very much."

"Then doesn't he love us too?" I asked worriedly.

"Why do you say that, Beta?"

"Why doesn't he take us there, too?" I sat by his chair, looking all put out.

"He only calls when he needs something from us," Ajoba replied, shifting uncomfortably.

"But can we see them?" I continued, stubbornly refusing to let go of this topic.

"No, we can't, not now. They become visible at night, as they become stars."

I seemed to be satisfied and sat cross-legged beside him on the floor, doodling in the mud with a stick, humming my favourite nursery rhyme, 'Twinkle, twinkle…'.

It was so peaceful now. It hadn't been so last month.

On Sunday afternoon, Ajoba had sat in the chair as usual and had fallen right through. He was so angry, his face had gone a peculiar shade of red. He had let out a string of oh so many words, and Aaji had come running out and closed my ears. Everyone tried their best not to laugh. I was the only one laughing out loud. It was with some difficulty that Aaji and my aunt had managed to pull him out.

An army-style inquisition followed thereafter, and the culprit was caught.

The wooden recliner had a cloth base, kept in place by slipping a wooden stick in the cloth fold. I had been playing and needed a sword to vanquish the demon—until I noticed the stick and seized my chance.

"Ajoba, I'll help you," I said, starting to untie his shoelaces, trying to make up for all the trouble I had caused.

"Oh, let it be, Beta, I'll do it myself," Ajoba said, dissuading me.

I ignored it and went ahead with the job. Knots were a fascination for me, and it took me quite some time to untie them whilst Ajoba looked indulgently. As the shoes came off, I pinched my nose in expectation.

"I told you don't touch them, now go and wash your hands," he reproached me.

Aaji placed a steaming hot cup of tea and a glass of water and went inside to prepare some snacks.

I followed Ajoba to the side of the house where an aluminium bucket of water and a tumbler were kept. A cool evening breeze blew away the napkin that Aaji had kept on the door latch.

"It's rained somewhere," he said, cupping his soaped hands as I poured some water on them.

"Ajoba, your feet are so dirty," I said.

The nails were so dry and cracked, and they needed a clipping.

He was washing his feet, rubbing one over the other. I poured the water over his nails, hoping the dirt collected under them would wash away. I kept on pouring the water on his feet until they looked cleaner.

They couldn't be his, I thought to myself. They were so clean, and the nails were clipped to perfection. So white and clean, they looked cold to the touch.

Some tear drops fell onto the flowers I placed on his feet. I was sixteen now, as I touched his feet and bid my last farewell. They chanted god's name as they picked up the makeshift wooden stretcher on their shoulders.

****

2. Hasinabi

The first time I heard her was when I was watering the garden. It was late in the morning in the month of May. The lane was quiet as people had taken refuge indoors with their coolers and fans. The sweltering heat was beginning to take its toll on me, too! I was about to turn off the tap and follow suit when I heard the song.

Hasan was strolling on the streets of pleasure. He was bored with it all. Once he had been a regular visitor, but now the scene was nauseatingly familiar. He had made up his mind to go back home when a melodious voice stopped him in his tracks.

That voice was so soulful. He looked up, expecting to see bright lights of a 'mehfil', but there was nothing of the sort. A single bulb glowed in the room. He started to climb the stairs but then hesitated and walked all the way back home, the voice still playing in his head. Home was a small room in a 'chawl'(a type of residential building) which he shared with two others who, like himself, had come to the big city looking for work. He shared the leftover biryani and unrolled the mattress. The last thing he vaguely remembered before falling asleep was his roommates teasing him about going to bed so early.

The next morning, he went to work at the 'Shabbir hotel' where he cut up vegetables and did odd jobs in the kitchen. When evening came, his feet took him to the same streets and the same house of the night before. He stood under the window in the street, waiting to hear the voice. Hasan went there night after night until he finally mustered the courage to climb the stairs and step into the room.

A young, beautiful girl sat alone on the floor in the room. She stopped singing on seeing him. Fear and disgust were the first emotions that appeared on her face before she hid them well with the most inviting look.

"Aaye Janab," she said.

But Hasan wasn't interested in this person; he wanted the girl he had chanced to see just as he entered. The real one, not this painted doll. It took Hasan weeks before he got to meet her. He would go there every evening just to sit before her and would request her to sing. Slowly, love blossomed in the streets of sin.

One day, Hasan asked her to marry him. The expression on her face he would never forget. They ran away and got married, and set up a house in a far-off place on the outskirts of a densely populated slum.

Here, the girl of the streets, Pakeezah, fondly named after a popular movie of olden times, became Hasinabi, a respected wife and mother of five children.

Hasinabi had blossomed rather bloated into a woman now, but Hasan still called her his Pakeezah, much to the amusement of his children, and she still blushed like a new bride.

Always taking care to dress up for her husband with henna in her hair and a fresh flower tucked in her bun.

The eldest daughter, Shaheen, was sixteen when Hasinabi delivered a baby boy, Nasir, who was mentally challenged. Hasan had a thing about retardation or any kind of handicap and his deep fear returned to haunt him. He started avoiding the child and often came late after work.

Over the years, Hasan had done well for himself. He had started his own small canteen outside the industrial area and was doing well. Initially, he had given some reason for his absence, but came home for food. At home, all the mess and the child's unkept appearance seemed to put him off. He would avoid the child's touch whenever he came to Hasan, calling him 'Abba'. Hasan had stopped coming home altogether and slept in his canteen.

Hasinabi had pleaded with him to return, but he avoided her touch altogether, fearing another child like Nasir. She cried herself to sleep every night. One day, on one of his weekly visits, when she had approached him, he had gotten so angry with her, calling her names and accusing her, saying the child wasn't his.

He had felt better having no part in bringing such a child into this world; he was not to blame, it was all Hasinabi's fault.

"You and your sins, all your past is coming back to you," he shouted at Hasinabi before banging the door shut.

She had run after him, crying out loud, "What will become of me? Have I not been a good wife and a mother?, its not my fault the child is yours, Hasan, please believe me!" but he didn't look back.

After a month, Hasan came early one morning, and her heart was filled with hope. She gave him a shy smile and blushed. Hasan was unmoved; he just kept the bundle of money on the doorstep and left without saying a word. As Nasir grew up, Hasinabi had to clean up after him. he roamed about the slum the whole day and came back home irritated and full of dirt and bruises.

"Everyone teases me and beats me up, Amma, tell me why," Nasir asked her with tears in his eyes, and Hasinabi had no answer for him, so she just took him close.

Hasinabi's hopes had died that day; she finally accepted that he wouldn't return. She waited and waited, the money came in regularly, but there was no sign of Hasan. Hasinabi was getting bored and restless. now her life had revolved around Hasan all these years, now just an empty ache remained. Her neighbor Asha worked as a maid in the building nearby. Hasinabi would watch her hurrying to work every day, and she envied her for her smartness; she wondered what earning one's own money felt like. One day, she mustered the courage and asked Asha hesitantly. Asha asked her if she was serious, for she was going to her native place for 15 days, and would she fill in for her then.

At first, Hasina panicked, but since it was just temporary, she finally relented and decided to give it a try. The first day, Asha introduced Hasinabi, and she was very awkward at work, but after a few days, she began to enjoy her routine. The disciplined life gave her a sense of purpose. At home, her daughter Shaheen now did all the household jobs, so she wasn't overburdened and started enjoying this sense of freedom.

Money was important, but she got to see the lives of the other half, to interact with them, and be a part of a world she had hitherto only dreamt of, even if it meant skirting around that invisible boundary which separates the classes. Thereafter, she found work in about four households, and the years just flew by. The first time she came to work in our house, she was wearing a gaudy pink sari, dangling earrings, and her orange henna hair with a big red rose in her bun. She was sixty years old then. I was in two minds about hiring her, but curiosity won hands over that and the fact that I had no maid for the past month. I asked after a few days what her husband did for a living when we both were enjoying a cup of tea.

She blushed to her hair roots, taking her sari 'pallu' in her mouth after giving me an almost toothless grin. "He runs a canting bai," she said proudly.

It took some further explanations to understand that she actually meant the canteen.

Hasinabi was a regular, sincere worker and didn't get offended if I scolded her for her repeated mistakes. She only needed a cup of tea, chapati, and she would request me to switch on the 'Vividh Bharati' radio channel, which played all old Hindi songs at around that time, and she was all energized. She would often hum along and seemed to have a nice voice. Another of her interests was gadgets; any new electronic equipment was bought, and Hasinabi was there in the forefront right from unloading to the demo.

One day, she came with a bowl of onion 'pakoras'.

"He makes these very well," she said shyly, "Do try some, memsahib."

"Has he come back now?" I asked, picking one pakora and popping it into my mouth, it was really tasty.

"Jab jawani main nahi aya aab budhape main kya ayega," she lamented(when he left me in my youth, why will he come to me now in my old age).

"He had come for my grandson's birthday," she explained.

One day, she came later than usual and was unusually quiet. I asked her what happened, and she seemed reluctant at first, but her tongue got the better of her.

"That Prithvi apartments lady accused me of stealing her gold earrings. She called the police, and I was called at the station for questioning. The policewoman slapped me quite hard, madam."

She lost that job, of course, and the earrings were not found in her house.

A few months later, I saw a trail of sugar fallen on the floor right from the kitchen outside the main door. I had my suspicions, but didn't want to make hasty decisions.

The next time, it was the tea powder. Then the smell of my perfume in the room and on her.

"Hasinabi, have you been doing something you shouldn't?" I spoke to her sternly one day.

She pleaded innocence, refused to admit anything, and kept changing the topic. I decided to give her one more chance.

Hasinabi would take the garbage to the corner dumpster every day after completing her household work. I decided to check it one day, finding some of the new soaps missing. The moment she stepped outside the house, I asked her to open the bin. She was hesitant at first, but finally had to give in to my insistent tone. In it were the missing soaps and some sugar in a plastic bag.

I couldn't trust her anymore. She cried and begged me to give her one more chance. But I asked her to stop coming to work.

Some ten to fifteen days later, I heard a familiar voice singing as I stood watering the garden one morning. I looked through the gates, and there was Hasina walking towards the recently built housing complex in a fluorescent green sari and a big red rose in her bun.

I smiled at her as she greeted me and asked me how I was. She had a spring in her step as if she were excited to start a new adventure.

Song: "Inhi logon ne leliya dupatta mera," she sang(these people have taken away my dupatta, my respect…).

****

3. The Outhouse

The bungalow was a double-storeyed, ugly cement structure, unpainted, unkempt; it was a sad, neglected place. It very much resembled its owners. The old couple's only son has settled abroad, and his visits have decreased from every year to once in two years to none over the past ten years. They used two rooms on the ground floor the rest they had let out to students to make ends meet.

The outhouse stood in the right-hand corner of the plot behind the bungalow. That's where we lived—Aunty, Uncle, and I. They couldn't have children of their own and had adopted me. I called them Aunty and Uncle.

I'm twelve years old now. My real father was Uncle's elder brother, who died of brain fever when I was two. My birth mother couldn't afford to raise all four of us children. I saw her now and then, but she felt more like a stranger to me.

I study in Class Six at the local government school—School Number Twenty-One. Aunty cooks and cleans for the elderly couple in the bungalow, while Uncle works as a night watchman and, during the day, as a salesperson at a shoe shop.

Next to the entrance, a small patch of land had been lovingly turned into a vegetable garden on one side, while wild white and pink roses bloomed freely on the other.

"Hello Tilotamma, any eggs today?" I asked our favourite brown hen. She sat regally in the three feet by four feet coop made of just mesh and some old wooden planks by my uncle, with five other hens and two cocks. The sale from the eggs went into a biscuit tin, 'for a rainy day,' aunty would say.

After washing my feet under the tap outside, I entered the house. A single room was divided into two rooms by an asbestos sheet. In the summer, the room became a furnace. The tin roof let in the rainwater in the monsoon and made us run helter-skelter for pots and pans of all shapes and sizes.

There was hardly any room to manoeuvre on entering the room, with the two iron beds and kitchen utensils placed in the opposite corners. The third corner had a sunken washing area, while the fourth had the door to the next room. The walls were damp with peeling green distemper, and I would peel off the cracked paint and spend hours imagining the pictures and figures that were revealed. This was my favourite pastime when Aunty took her afternoon nap.

There were some old-fashioned wooden pegs to hang things on. I used the one above the bed to swing. One day, the peg broke, carrying both the bags and me right onto the teacups and saucers, which my aunt had been setting on the tray.

It had been a disaster of sorts with the guests waiting inside for their tea and no teacups to serve them in. Aunty had been livid with anger, and I had run away from the crime scene and hid next to the chicken coop. The guests were told about the incident, and they had a good laugh. Tea was served in the glasses used to serve water. I had not been given any tea that day.

The room inside had a cupboard and chairs for the guests. An old steel lamp with an ugly plastic lampshade, which looked like a skirt, and was totally out of place amongst the tin folding chairs. But aunty was proud of it. Her employer, Mrs Shah, had parted with it a year ago because it had gone out of fashion.

Beyond the house, there were acres and acres of barren land. This was home to the nomads, gypsies and other unruly characters who hung about there, making it an unsafe area after dark.

The compound barbed wire was bent out of shape in many places, and many times, small things went missing day after day. Pigs, goats would wander in and trample the rose bushes and eat the vegetables. Some people complained to the police, and then there would be a cleanup drive—suddenly, all the gypsies would be gone.

Things stayed quiet for a few days, but soon enough, a tent would appear, then another, and the settlers would return. By now, even the police had stopped paying attention.

During the summer holidays, the students went home, and the place fell silent. Aunty would jump at every little harmless sound. The heat grew unbearable, and Uncle wanted to sleep outdoors. But Aunty wouldn't hear of it— she swore she'd seen a snake the week before. So, every night, we baked under the tin roof with all the doors locked. If Aunty had her way, even the windows would've been shut tight, if not for Uncle's loud and stubborn objections.

"It's not the robbers but you who'll kill us all with suffocation !" he shouted at her.

One such summer's night, I got up in the middle of the night, drenched in sweat. There was no electricity, and the absence of the sound of the table fan was the first thing I noticed. The silence was stifling. It was pitch dark, and I couldn't see a thing. At first, I thought I had gone blind and opened my mouth to scream when a hand closed over my mouth, and I would have fainted in terror had it not been for my aunt's familiar voice.

After a while, as my eyes got adjusted to the darkness, I could see my uncle's form standing to one side of the window, looking out. Aunt and I crept up to him and watched with our eyes wide open in terror. About five to six men tall hefty men wearing loincloths, were carrying away our chicken coop. I was terrified, my aunt just hugged me closer and kept her hand over my mouth the whole time.

We couldn't go back to sleep after that and just sat huddled together in the dark, talking in whispers. Aunt was bemoaning her fate and vowed never to keep another coop again. Her biscuit tin wouldn't hear a coin's jingle for some time. I was devastated to lose my best friend Tillotama. Two weeks later, we had built another coop and one by one had bought five to six chicks again.

The next summer, the old lady was taken ill, and aunt and uncle rushed her to the hospital. She came home ten days later but suffered another stroke a month later. Aunt looked after her; she fed her rice, kanji, tea, and milk with a spoon. She gave her sponge baths and carried her bed pans, all with a smile on her face, never once uttering a word of disgruntlement. The old man was very grateful to my aunt and tried giving her money, but she refused, saying she would not take money looking after her own mother.

"I've already got the satisfaction," she told him. "Please don't take that away from me by offering money. That's all I have, Saheb."

After the old lady's death, the old man seemed to have given up on life. His son hadn't even come for his mother's funeral. He moped around the house and even stopped his regular morning walks. Aunt and Uncle coaxed him to eat food and take his medicines. I would often visit him after school and chat about the school when he asked me how my day went. For a short period, he seemed to have that old spark in his eyes, but he would quickly lapse into his dark zone when we left him at night after dinner.

It was the third year after the old lady's death when the old man did not get up one morning. The doctor had come in the previous evening as he had been feeling uneasy, but all seemed normal for the time being, and he had slept peacefully after dinner. Uncle did all the running around; he spent his own savings to complete the religious rites and pooja, and even lit the funeral pyre, as once again the son had not come.

A fortnight later, the old man's lawyer came to inspect the premises. By then, my uncle had already started searching for another place. Rooms in better localities were far too expensive, and the affordable ones were found only on the fringes of the slum area.

Uncle and aunt had been reluctant to go there, but the moment they saw the lawyer, they came to the unhappy decision. Uncle placed our best chair outside at his disposal, and Aunt brought a glass of water and stood respectfully at a distance.

After a long, awkward silence, the lawyer said, "You will have to leave the outhouse now."

"Yes, sir, we will move out in two or three days," Uncle said with his head bent low.

"Where will you go?" the lawyer asked.

"Sir, the vasti (slum area) in Ramwadi behind the railway line," uncle answered timidly.

It was then that the lawyer burst out laughing and got up to pat my uncle on the back. Uncle and aunt looked up, bewildered. We all thought the man had taken leave of his senses. Saying this, the lawyer opened his briefcase and removed a sheet of paper

This is the deceased's will, which he made four years ago, and you are to get the bungalow and the rest of his assets. Uncle sat down on the ground holding his head in his hands. Aunt screamed, almost fainted, and fell down at the lawyer's feet.

Many years later, the bungalow was named after the old man, and my uncle and aunt ran an old-age home and did manage to renovate the outhouse and continued to live there.

****

4. Conference

"You're very sexy, you know," said the husky voice.

"Thanks for the compliment, it's the first time anyone has said that so…so very openly," said the voice softly.

The conference was in full swing. After a series of long, boring lectures, the video clippings and slide shows were going on. The room was in total darkness, and everyone was dozing off.

"Let's go outside now," Husky whispered," No one will even notice."

"But we might step on someone's toes," started Sexy," Um…let's do it anyway, this slide show is putting me to sleep," continued Sexy after a moment's thought.

A second later, they were out in the cool air, walking towards the sea without even thinking about it.

"It's so beautiful here, so peaceful, wish I could stay here forever," said Sexy, full of emotion." I love the sea, it's so dynamic, so powerful, yet the sound of the waves is so soothing," said Sexy, sighing.

"Yes, you're right! Here, the three elements of nature meet, wind, water, and the earth, and that meeting is pure magic," Husky stated

"Let's sit here on the sand," Sexy suggested," A bonfire would surely complete the picture."

"I've smuggled some beer out," Husky said, holding the bottle up triumphantly.

"You think of everything," Sexy said appreciatively, eyeing the bottle.

They became quiet, suddenly. It was a companionable silence. Words were not necessary between them. Each was aware of the other's presence, but there was no awkwardness. The cool breeze and the warm rays of the moon brought mixed feelings. Tomorrow was the last day of the conference.

'Goa' was a memorable experience. It had brought them together.

Husky reached out to hold Sexy's hand and squeezed it as though reading the others' thoughts.

"What next?'' Sexy whispered sadly.

Husky said, taking Sexy close," We have a whole night before us, it will last us a lifetime."

"Let's go up to the room," so saying, Husky got up, brushing the sand off his clothes and holding out a hand to Sexy.

The empty beer bottles lay there among the sands reflecting the moonlight while Husky and Sexy went into a world of their own.

The leaves of the coconut trees rustled restlessly, reflecting the restlessness within.

It was their last night together, and there was a new urgency in their love as if there was no tomorrow. It was true there would be no tomorrows. They had decided that. It could not be.

Their eyes were red in the morning. They hadn't slept a wink.

Hardly looking at each other, they dressed hurriedly, trying hard not to touch each other. The air was heavy, and their hearts were too. The bright sunny beach outside could not drive away the gloom settled in that room. Even the waves seemed to say, F-I-N-I-S-H, FI-N-I-S-H.

"Have you packed your bags?" Husky said in a strained voice,' The plane leaves at 4.00 PM, we'll have to leave immediately after the last seminar."

Sexy just managed to nod. They avoided each other's eyes as they picked up their folders and walked towards the conference room. Everyone was settling into their seats.

"Hello," Mr Bakshi said, then knowingly winking at them, he added," You people seemed to have quite a night, Na."

Sexy took a sharp breath and turned pale.

Bakshi continued," Too many beer bottles, Na, enjoy you're still young."

Husky let out his breath slowly," Got to be careful .", Husky thought to himself.

At last, it was over; they shook hands with some acquaintances and checked out of the hotel. They shared a taxi to the airport. Throughout the journey to Mumbai, both were lost deep in their own thoughts. It was the same one," What now?".

The journey was uneventful, and the plane landed in Mumbai. After completing the formalities, they walked out to the lounge.

Husky was jolted from his deep trance. "Daddy,'' a high-pitched voice broke into his thoughts. He looked up to see his nine-year-old son run towards him.

"Sonu, wait, don't run." Maya, his wife, made an unsuccessful attempt to restrain him.

Husky gathered his son close and held him tightly as though his very life depended on it.

He glanced up and caught Sexy's eyes, then quickly looked away, answering his son's query.

"Hi, sexy, you look tired, honey."

Sexy turned towards the direction of the voice and watched his beautiful, very pregnant wife walk towards him.

"She was so beautiful," Sexy thought as she rested her hands protectively on her belly, her eyes twinkling with laughter as she opened her arms wide to give him an awkward hug.

"They say love knows no bounds—but it does."

****

5. Shani Neecham

"You have a Rajyog in your kundali, but," he proclaimed sonorously, concentrating on the sheet of paper before him.

In the interim long pause, I managed to look around the well-furnished house, "He must do well."I thought to myself.

From where I sat daydreaming, it looked like an asymmetrical design. As the voice droned on and on, I shifted my attention to the pattern on the curtain.

"Your Shani is neecham," he was saying. *"His what is what?"* That's when I seemed to snap out of my daydream.

"The Saturn is not in its strong position and is housed with Shukra (Venus) in the seventh house," he turned his head towards me disapprovingly.

"Do you have problems in your marriage?" he asked, narrowing his eyes as if trying to bore into our heads and our very souls.

If not before, we definitely would now, I thought to myself.

I wanted to ask about my career developments, but Sameer, my husband, was worried about his; it doesn't seem to be going in any direction.

The long and short of it was that nothing moved—it all just stayed stuck. Nothing ever seems to happen in my life. Half my energy is spent just trying to recover from setbacks. For the past four years, it's felt like one pitfall after another.

"Hmm," the astrologer managed to say, ponderously struggling to drag himself away from the seventh house.

I observed him surreptitiously as he studied the chart in another corner. He must have found the usual bits—career, money—boring. But the seventh house? Now that was truly interesting: prying into someone's private life. Most astrologers seem obsessed with this house, as if it's their sacred duty to bring it up—assuming, of course, that the person is too shy to ask about it themselves. This was the fifth astrologer we had visited for the same problem.

We had started with a nonbeliever's scorn when we showed our horoscope for the very first time at a friend's insistence. We got hooked on these visits somewhere along the line.

From a practical point of view, we were comfortably off. Both were educated and had a successful love marriage for the past decade with two wonderful children. But we wanted the elusive words attached before our names, 'successful'.

Mark Twain once said that 'All you needed in this life is ignorance and confidence, and then success is sure'. We lacked in the latter and had oodles of the former.

I read all I could on astrology, borrowing books from my parents, who must have gone through a similar star-searching phase of their own. Now the books were found in the upstairs room, the diwan all dusty and long forgotten. I often wondered what it was we looked for. What was that empty feeling we hadn't hitherto experienced?

We had been content to let life pass us by—watching friends and even former subordinates climb the ladder of success, zooming past us in their latest four-wheeled drives. Meanwhile, we balanced bags full of diapers, milk bottles, and our two kids on our rickety two-wheeler, ferrying them across town to my mother's place before heading off to work—me to my part-time job, and my husband all over the city, and sometimes even beyond it.

For most of our lives, we moved like zombies—half-awake, going through the motions. Now, it feels like we've finally entered the rat race. We stepped gingerly onto the tracks, hopeful that life would carry us forward. But the worst part? We just stood there—paralysed— while everything and everyone rushed past. We watched and listened as all kinds of people went by, even those we once thought of as laid-back or lost causes—repeaters, so-called losers from our past—now focused, successful, and wealthy.

We were academically good, and people had expected us to be successful, but there is no such correlation; we were beginning to learn it the hard way.

Having gone through the usual practical questions and still finding success elusive, we began making occasional visits to astrologers. At first, it was in the hope of finding some answers; these days, it feels more like shopping for variety.

Actually, we still don't know when it started, but our sporadic visits to the astrologer became a regular shopping spree. Let's just see what he or she says.

The one who presently sat before us had his first, last, and middle names, which actually sounded like first names. After three visits, we still hadn't figured out which one to use, and I think we've been addressing him by his father's name all these days. Last time he had asked my husband, Sameer, to start using 'Neelam'(Blue sapphire) stone in a chain. It had not adversely affected us after about a week of keeping it in the wallet, so we were advised to get it set in a gold chain. After soaking it in raw milk overnight and chanting the 'Shani stotra', Sameer adorned this chain on the first hora (early morning) on a Saturday.

I, too, had been advised to wear a pearl. At first, the astrologer suggested a diamond—25 to 30 cents, set in platinum. But one look at my face, and he quickly offered a more affordable alternative. I'm convinced these astrologers take a glance at your mode of transport before recommending a gemstone. Still, I was secretly thrilled at the thought of being told to wear a diamond!

Four years later, we found ourselves visiting him again for a reassessment, having seen two other astrologers in the meantime. The second one, a sharp-tongued woman we consulted after a string of mishaps that year, had advised us to remove the Shani pendant. Her reasoning was simple: Shani delays everything, and if it's already weak in your kundali, why strengthen it further?

"Do you want to be a cog in your own wheel?" she had asked.

This was a different point of view—completely new to us—and we were excited. That was just last month. But still, the void remained, and a few minor incidents occurred almost immediately after removing the chain. And so, we found ourselves back here once again.

"This is worse than gambling or any other addiction," I told Sameer the other day, but we called up the astrologer for an appointment anyway. It hadn't been ours for that matter, what started out as a, just let's see what he says, he is good, and look how he helped us, became a never-ending journey for us.

"I don't think it's an obsession. I think it's just a reassurance—our quest for some answers," Sameer said, trying to console me, though he didn't sound convinced.

"Thank God we don't go before every little event, asking what colour to wear and doing all those poojas like Bhaskar Uncle," I said happily, copying the kundali onto the last page of my diary. I had already misplaced it twice and was planning to get a computerized one next time.

"But they are benefitting from all this," Sameer retorted irritably.

"Then what about us? Haven't we found the right guruji yet?" I asked worriedly.

Sameer didn't answer me, but was lost in thought.

"Maybe there is no such perfect formula for this success thing," Sameer answered in a small, dejected voice.

"Maybe it's not in our fate after all," I said, feeling the clouds of depression gathering.

"Look at Manoj see how he prospered and we had started about the same time." he continued, "Rohan has already left for the UK, I think this is not for us we must stop, what do you think? Let it come to us when it must or not," he asked questioningly.

I nodded my head in agreement.

"After this last visit to the astrologer your brother recommended," I answered quickly.

"Alright," Sameer replied readily. "As you wish." He got up to get ready, almost eager.

****

6. Autumn Leaves

"Give us four each," said the frail old lady eyeing the 'Gulab Jamuns' greedily.

The others cast a furtive look in the direction of the warden. I quickly caught on to their subtle message. I placed four jamuns on each plate. One rolled over the chipped part of the glass plate and landed in the rice. I apologised, but the old lady just gave me a toothless smile.

Her hair was snowy white, tied up with a thin black ribbon, her fair skin lined with many wrinkles resembling an intricate web. She looked like a foreigner, I thought to myself.

The meal consisted of rice and watery dal. A few had bottles of pickle or chutney, their lids stubborn enough to need a helping hand. Some were sharing their goodies with the others, who were not so fortunate. The snow-haired lady looked wistfully at them, but the warden's warning look was enough to put that wish out the window.

Then, catching my eye, the warden explained, "Hypertension, you know, she's had a massive heart attack already," she continued as if the subject under discussion wasn't present.

The bungalow wherein they were housed was the legacy of the 'British Raj', the old faded sign said 'Autumn leaves', an apt name, I thought. The garden surrounding it had huge peepal and banyan trees, and the flowerbeds were full of weeds. The building itself was single-storeyed with thick stone walls with a high sloping roof.

The room we sat in was a living cum a dining room with an old black television set perched on a rickety wooden table. The furniture consisted of overstuffed, oversized sofas with faded flowers that had seen better days. The spring underneath was making its presence felt. I tried shifting my weight around to find a comfortable spot, but there were many of its kin.

The telephone rang, breaking the awkward silence, and the warden seemed relieved to get up. The conversation was curt, and her face became grave. She sat near me and was quiet for a moment.

An inmate who had collapsed last evening after dinner had passed away.

"Let them finish their lunch and their afternoon naps, then I will tell them during tea time," she whispered.

"Who was that?" the snowy-haired woman asked, receiving no reply. She continued, "Was that about Mabel? Is she okay?" She went on relentlessly

"Why don't you eat, Mrs Chapman? It was just the grocers," she said in a soothing tone.

Unconvinced and worried, Mrs Chapman continued eating silently.

One by one, each of the ten ladies left the table and made their way slowly to the wash basins. It took them another fifteen minutes to settle into the sofas with some difficulty.

Mrs Chapman was the unofficial spokesperson of the group, I guessed, as she asked me my name, profession, and the occasion of my visit. It was on special occasions that people came to visit the old homes. The visits were infrequent and far between.

I told her it was my mother's birthday, though in truth, it was the day she had passed away four years ago. But I didn't have the heart to say that and burden them with talk of death. After performing the pooja on her first death anniversary, I found I preferred to mark the day by visiting old-age homes and spending time with the senior citizens.

"Let's sing for her," Mrs Chapman said enthusiastically, and the others joined in clapping their hands, singing' happy birthday to Sadhana, happy birthday…"

I had been feeling like a fraud lying to them, but now I was glad I had, they seemed so happy. I felt as if their joyous singing had brought my mother back to life. I so miss her now.

I thanked them all, and the warden began introducing them. I couldn't remember all the details, but one of them was a doctor, Soudamini Joshi, in her 80's she was hard of hearing and seemed to have switched off from this world. Once, an esteemed doctor, a renowned surgeon, sat slouched in the chair, twiddling her thumbs and mumbling to herself. Having chosen to remain unmarried and serve society, she had no close relative to visit her or mourn her death.

Banoo, a seventy-year-old Parsi lady, used to teach music and elocution in a renowned school nearby. Having suffered a stroke twice, she had difficulty moving her right arm and leg. She walked about, dragging her feet along the floor. She loved to talk, but one had difficulty trying to decipher her slurred speech. Her only son had left for the United States and was a somewhat brilliant, forgetful scientist. He seemed to have forgotten the very existence of his mother. Though the money came in regularly, he hadn't bothered to visit her even once in ten years. Occasionally, her niece would stop by on New Year's Day with a box of sweets.

Mrs. Chapman was English by birth but raised in Mussoorie. Her father had served in the army, and her husband had been in the British army stationed in India. Their children had moved to England long ago, but the couple had chosen to stay on here. After her husband's death, Mrs. Chapman felt it was her duty to fulfil his last wishes.

The bungalow that now housed the old-age home had once been their family home. They had begun by taking in a few lonely, elderly friends. Before long, it became a full-fledged old-age home. Over time, occupancy dwindled from thirty to ten—partly due to natural losses, and partly from lack of funds.

The place ran solely on charity, and some inmates were lucky enough to have their relatives paying regular fees for their upkeep. After a few minutes of chatting, Mrs Chapman invited me to her room. I hesitated, but seeing the warden's encouraging smile, I went along.

Her room was tiny but comfortable. There was a beautiful mahogany dressing table and a four-poster bed. There was no place for a chair, so I remained standing. Come sit, my child, she said, patting the bed, and I obeyed. I looked around the neat and cosy place. That one room housed her whole life. All the objects that sparked joy, probably.

Mrs Chapman hobbled to the dresser. I noticed she wore a blue sock on her left foot and a red one on her right. Her legs had a network of varicose veins. Giving me a handful of chocolates, she sat chatting with us, asking us many questions and recounting the many anecdotes of her youth.

I lost track of time, and it was nearly three by the time I left. I had caused her to miss her afternoon nap. As I walked towards the gate, I heard the clinking of teacups, and the aroma of tea wafted across to me. I looked back one last time and saw the yard full of yellow autumn leaves, but it made a pretty picture.

****

7. Raw Mangoes

The scorching heat was too much to bear. Even the tar on the road appeared to be melting with the heat of the afternoon sun. Not a soul dared to appear on the streets. The dogs had found cool places under parked cars and under the staircase of the Housing Board building. The alleys had a haunted look, the sparrows and crows too didn't bother to chirp and stay put in the shady trees, which were few and far between.

Savitri walked quickly, head bent and covered with a thin chiffon 'odhani'(a long, scarf-like cloth draped over the head and shoulders, often worn with traditional Indian attire), her slippers making a flip-flop noise as she reached the grocery shop. She had to bend her head and waist to enter the shop, for the shutters were half closed down to protect the shopkeeper's eyes from the afternoon sun's glare.

There was no one at the counter, and a rickety fan whirled on the ceiling loudly, rotating the same hot air over and over again.

"Gogaramji!" Savitri called out loudly. "Are you there?"

There was a sound of plastic 'dabbas' (boxes) and a curse, as first a backside and then a head emerged behind the counter.

"Sleeping kya?", Savitri teased the shopkeeper. "I want a packet of ' mehendi', castor sugar half a kilo, and another one kilo 'maida'(white flour)."

"You've been troubling me since yesterday morning, coming every half an hour, why don't you make a list and take all you want once and for all?." Gogaram grumbled and rubbed his eyes.

Savitri watched in disgust at the dried-up drool at the angle of his mouth.

"How are the marriage preparations going?" Gogaram asked, deftly packing the caster sugar in newspaper and tying it with string that, mysteriously, seemed to stay in place despite no visible knots being made.

"They are going on and on and on," Savitri answered in a bored voice, putting the packets in her cloth bag. "Write the amount in our account, chacha," she added as she bent her head once again to go out, almost blinded by the bright sunlight outside.

Skipping all the twenty yards to her house, she hardly felt the sun as she dreamt about the wedding and getting excited as she drew near the house door, hearing all the hustle and bustle within.

"What took you so long?" chided her mother and took the bag from her as soon as she entered the courtyard."The sweets must be ready by five and Rani has to put that mehendi on her hair, only four more hours left for them to come." She seemed to be talking to herself as she entered the kitchen calling out to her elder sister Mala.

"It's getting late, we must hurry, they'll be coming soon," was all she had been saying for the past fifteen days.

There were people everywhere. The courtyard was full of 'charpoys'(wooden coir woven cots), with men and women of all sizes and ages lounging about doing absolutely nothing. Shanta Aaji was sitting on one amidst everyone, one leg folded at the knee, cutting the betelnuts with an ancient nut cracker into small pieces for the 'paan'. Her mouth was black with the 'mishri'(roasted tobacco) she had applied to her teeth, her daily afternoon ritual.

She called out to Dhonduram, the old servant, adjusting her saree pallu back over her head with her now dried, mishri-stained blackened finger.

"Have the marigold garlands been put up yet? Have you finished stringing the flowers?" she bellowed.

"Ha, Baisaab," Dondu murmured, standing before her with his head bowed. It was only some time later that she realized he was still there.

"Now what do you think you're doing just standing there? Come on, move! Ask the cook if the *laddoos* are ready," she yelled at the nearly deaf man.

Savitri gazed at the bright marigold and mango-leaf garlands strung all around the house. The mango leaves, a symbol of prosperity, were considered auspicious. The dark green ones glistened in the sunlight, though a few had turned brown, and someone had even snapped off the tender new ones. She skipped toward the kitchen, but just then, Shanta Aaji called out, asking her to fetch a glass of water from inside.

Savitri made a face behind her back, then reluctantly went inside. She came out with a brass *tambya* (a traditional water container with a wide mouth and rounded body) and *phulpatra* (a small, curved drinking vessel used to sip water) and handed them to Aaji. As Aaji gulped down the water—half of it running down her chin—she signaled Savitri to wait.

"Ask Malati and Vidya to make some rangoli designs at the doorstep."

Savitri decided not to go anywhere near Aaji—she wouldn't let her sit for even a minute, and her stomach had begun to growl. She slipped into the kitchen, opened the metal tins, and took two laddoos, watching the huge iron vessels bubbling away over the wood fires set beneath them. They looked like a witch's cauldron, ready to roast small, fat children.

Savitri's imagination ran wild. A cold wave of fear ran down her spine. Shaking off her scary thoughts, she drank a glass of water and ran off to her sister's room.

All her cousin sisters had gathered around Rani, her sister, and they were giggling and teasing her, and her ears were turning red. She was looking so beautiful, so different from the 'Taai' she was used to seeing. The yellow saree with the bright red border looked great on her, but she seemed like a stranger somehow. Savitri entered the room and went to sit on one of the trunks in the corner of the room, eating her second laddoo, watching all the proceedings unnoticed. Everywhere, there were packed trunks and boxes filled with clothes and utensils.

"Oh! What a mess," thought Savitri.

All Tai's friends were gathered around her, admiring her saree and jewellery. 'Aaji', 'Aai', and some other women entered the room; they all made a big hustle and bustle and cleared the center of the room.

"Come, girls, we have to pound some 'haldi', turmeric, and apply the paste on Rani," Aaji said.

Aaji put some turmeric and 'kumkum'(a red powder traditionally applied on the forehead by married Hindu women)on the stone pounding vessel and started pounding the turmeric roots and singing in her high-pitched voice. All the other ladies put their right hands to Aajis and touched each other, forming a human chain. The singing went on for another ten minutes, and then milk and water were added to the haldi. The ladies then applied the paste one by one with a leaf from her legs to her face. They took her to the bathroom where each woman poured a mug full of water on her head, to which were added 'neem' leaves and rose petals, to ward off evil and give her a lovely rosy perfume. She was left to bathe by herself, then her hair was dried over the smoke made with 'dhoop' incense and 'ajwain' on a bucket full of heated coals. Aai and Kaku dried her hair. The turmeric paste was put aside to be put on the groom

"Savitri, everyone, go out now! We have to dress up *Taai*!" Saying this, we were all shooed out of the room.

" They are telling her the secrets of marriage," someone said and giggled.

"What could that be?" Savitri wondered, trying her very best to listen through the crack in the door. But She couldn't hear anything significant—just some mumbling and giggling. She eventually got bored and ran out to play with Janhavi, her cousin, who was a year younger than her. She would be fourteen in four months.

Malati and Vidya were busy making the rangolis, deftly making designs on the ground. A border of flowers, 'kalash', 'swastik', and some dots were made with a white coloured powder. Colourful rangoli was then used to fill up the designs just like colouring with crayons. I thought.

They gathered their long skirts and ran all the way to the mango groves, racing each other and laughing till their sides hurt.

Climbing high up into the trees, they sat on a branch and plucked and ate the raw mangoes. Savitri loved them so much. Thus, they sat for half an hour discussing the marriage festivities, school, and whatnot, only a teenager can find important.

Then Savitri climbed down. All that sherbet (a sweet, cooling drink made from fruit or flower syrup) had left her uncomfortable, and she needed to find a quiet spot. She walked toward the big boulder, glancing around to make sure no one was nearby.

Just as she turned to leave, she spotted an almost-ripe mango hanging low—just within reach, or so she thought. Savitri jumped high, but in vain. Just looking at it made her mouth water.

Savitri jumped high, but in vain. Just looking at it made her mouth water.

"Do you want any help?" Savitri jumped with a start and turned toward the source of the deep voice.

"Oh, Pawar uncle," she said, relieved to recognize the familiar face who often visited their house and sat smoking 'beedis' on the 'charpoy' with her dad.

"Uncle, could you help me please?" Savitri asked him eagerly.

"Sure, but you'll have to give me a taste of your raw mangoes first," Pawar Uncle said, smiling at her.

"O.K.," Savitri said readily, not seeing the look in Pawar's eyes.

Pawar Uncle held the mango out in his outstretched hand and asked her to come and get it. She stepped forward eagerly.

But as she reached for it, he caught her wrist. She looked up, a little surprised—and then she saw his eyes.

Something's not right was the only thought that crossed her mind. She tried to snatch her hand back, but he tightened his grip.

"You're beautiful, you know," Pawar Uncle was saying, gently pushing her back toward the tree trunk. "Just like the raw mango."

Before she could react, he stifled her scream with his hand, his fingers moving quickly to undo her blouse buttons, his touch invading, wrong.

She thrashed about trying to escape, her eyes wide with fear as he brought his mouth closer to her breasts. She felt sick, so angry with herself, so dirty. His hands were under her skirts now.

She was terrified. What was he doing? This wasn't right, not right at all, was all she could think.

"Savitri," a voice called out, breaking into her thoughts."What's taking you so long?" Janhavi was calling out.

Pawar got away with a start, "I thought you were alone," he said reproachfully,

"We'll meet again," he added with a smile and went off hurriedly and disappeared in the grove soon out of sight.

Savitri sank down against the tree, as though paralyzed.

"What happened ?" Janhavi said urgently and rushed forward as she saw her sitting on the ground.

"I fell down from the tree," Savitri managed to mumble, doing up her buttons with trembling hands. "Oh, are you hurt badly?" Janhavi said, not really looking at her.

Savitri was rocking back and forth.

"Now see this mango!" Janhavi cried out. "You selfish one, you were going to eat it all by yourself, weren't you? Here, let's share it."

She prattled on, busy tearing off the skin, the juice dripping down her chin as she held the other half out to Savitri.

Savitri felt sick just looking at it." I don't want it, I'm not feeling well, let's go home."

"Do you want this other raw mango then?" Janhavi was happy to barter.

"No!" Savitri shouted, running toward the house, tears streaming down her face. "I hate raw mangoes!"

****

8. Yellappa

L-O-N-D-O-N-London, London, London, all of us screamed.

Manu, hey Manya, you're out, O.K," Sonu was accusing me.

"No I'm not, I didn't move an inch, neither did I show my teeth, you're cheating, cheater –cock," I said emphatically making all sorts of monkey faces.

Then came Neelu, Abhi, and Sapna demanding to know exactly what was wrong. I stood there, tears streaming down my face.

I didn't cheat, I didn't lie," I said, brushing aside a fresh flow of tears with the back of my hand. I saw scornful faces and went red with anger, stamping my feet. I ran out of the garden and sat on a doorstep watching everyone play. I was feeling very dejected and lost.

"I've no friends," I said aloud, "Everyone's mean and I hate them all."

"What's that?" I said, turning around. I was sure I had heard a knock on the door next to which I sat.

But that's locked, I said to myself. I stared at the door, perplexed, standing a little away just in case. Then a soft noise came again.

"Who's that ?" I asked in a small, trembling voice. I went near the door, mustering up my courage, I pushed in the letter box lid on the door gingerly.

A pair of black eyes stared back at me. I blinked and fell back in surprise.

"Who are you?"I asked. But no answer came forth.

"Don't be scared," I said, trying to reassure the person sitting inside. "I am your friend, my name is Manu."

No answer.

"Why are you locked inside?" I asked. Just as I was about to say something more, my mom called out to me for lunch.

I hurriedly bid him—or her—I mean, the eyes, goodbye and ran home.

I came to the same house the next day and the day after the next day too, always bringing biscuits, sweets, and paratha, all hidden in my shirt pockets.

The third day, a small hand came out of the letterbox and took the sweets. There was silence for some time. I looked at the letterbox with wonder.

Then the voice started talking, "I want to get out, please help," in vernacular language but disjointed words which

I didn't understand, "I want to go home." The voice continued in a soft voice.

My mouth dried up, and I whispered right back.

"I will surely help you out, but why are you locked inside like this?"

I told my father everything that evening as soon as he came back from work. He was so shocked at first that he could barely say a word, and Mom just sat down on the sofa, stunned. Dad contacted the police and gave them the necessary information.

Yellappa, that was his name, was freed. He was burning with fever and was too weak to even sit up properly without support. The police filed a case against his employers, Mr and Mrs Rahi, for child labour and torture. We had to admit him to a hospital for his fever and malnourishment for a few days.

The next day, I overheard Dad telling Mom his story. He stayed in a small village in the state of Karnataka. His mother was the only earning member of his family, had been ill. Yellappa had lost his father at a very young age. He had two younger siblings and no money or food in the house. Almost everything that could be sold or pawned had already been given away.

Yellappa's mother's condition was worsening day by day. Yellappa knew he had to find work. He was ready to do anything, almost anything to save his dying mother.

That's why when he came to know that some people were looking for a house boy, he jumped at that chance. A light of hope kindled in his heart, and better days would come soon now. Yellappa had come to the city not knowing what lay in store for him.

Mrs Rahi, his employer, turned out to be a cruel and heartless lady. She made him work like a donkey day in and day out, always hovering around, ready to beat him up whenever he showed signs of getting tired. While going to work, she locked him in the house, taking care to lock the kitchen too, keeping only stale chapati and onion on his plate. Even dogs were fed properly! Yellappa was made to sleep in the verandah in the rains and winter with only a thin, torn sheet to cover him. He didn't get clothes, and his wages were non-existent, whenever he had asked for them. Mrs Rahi would get very angry and would prick his fingertips and put a hot tava on his head.

He could not ask for help as he didn't know the local language and was closely guarded by Mrs Rahi, who made sure he did not talk to anybody. Somehow, he bore everything for his mother's sake. If only Mrs Rahi would give him money, and somehow he could send it home for his mother's medicines and food for the little ones. He felt totally helpless, like a trapped animal.

I sat out stunned, thinking, "How could anyone be so cruel? This woman must be a witch." My childlike mind couldn't possibly understand all this. I wish I were strong enough to hit her back. Poor Yellappa!

We visited him in the hospital every day with food and picture books, and after nearly a week, he was fit to travel.

Dad decided to take him personally to his village. It took seven hours to reach it. Yellappa's eyes lit up as we turned into his village. On reaching there, we were struck by poverty; no wonder there were so many cases of child exploitation. It stood there, forlorn and forgotten, a shadow of what it once was. The place looked empty, neglected—almost abandoned.

"Amma," Yellappa half sobbed, half shouted as he ran toward the house. The door creaked open with a gust of wind. Yellappa's footsteps slowed down.

"Your mother is gone, my son," someone was saying, "she was asking for you till the very end."

She died just five days after you left. We all stood shocked, rooted to the ground. Yellappa's world had fallen to pieces. He clutched the pillar, needing all the support he could get from it. He sat down slowly. One of the neighbours had been looking after his younger siblings these past three months, and they came with them now running towards their elder brother, crying out aloud.

"Come with us, Yellappa. We'll take care of you. You can stay with us," I chattered, not fully understanding the gravity of the situation, but desperately trying to comfort my friend.

He shook his head and looked at me, "No, I can't, brother." he looked towards his siblings, his eyes were different, like a grown-up he hugged me close with tears in his eyes.

The village elders had decided to adopt these children and take care of them. Dad quietly slipped a bundle of notes into Yellappa's hand as he patted him on his head.

There was nothing more I could do, I turned slowly to go, brushing aside my tears. Our car started, and I looked back. I could see Yellappa standing at his doorstep. A cloud of dust enveloped him, and I saw him no more.

****

9. Dirty Linen

Minal bent down to pick another shirt to hang up on the line. The clothespin in place, she reached for another one. Standing back, she watched the clothes just like a connoisseur standing before his favourite painting in an art museum. She had cleaned all her husband's shirts— one couldn't trust a dhobi nowadays. That new whitener had worked wonders; the clothes actually looked like the ones shown in television commercials..

Now, dusting, and a cup of tea, she would read the morning paper. It was nearly noon now, and she smiled to herself. The cupboards were the last on today's list. These one-gram gold bangles looked good, she thought, peering closely to see the designs in an advertisement column in the newspaper. This was good, she said to herself as she took a sip of her tea. This was 'me' time.

After fifteen minutes, she rose refreshed to tackle the cupboard. She literally pushed all the clothes out of the cupboard onto the floor and sat cross-legged. Ironing, mending, giving away, and not sure the piles were increasing, a scrap of paper fell out of a shirt pocket as she folded it.

At first, she dismissed it as a bill, but a tiny heart-shaped drawing in one corner caught her attention, and she picked it up to get a closer look with a smile, probably one of their ancient love notes, she thought. From S to A with lots of love. See you at eight tomorrow. This seemed weird, Minal thought to herself.

The writing wasn't familiar, and whats with the S. The A could be Atul her husband, she kept it back in the shirt pocket dismissing it as a doodle but a tiny niggling doubt crept in. She worked like an automaton for the rest of the day. The kids came home, and then there was a whirl of activity: homework, milk, and she put them to sleep. Atul had gone on a tour to some important office work in Bangalore and would be back tomorrow.

She couldn't sleep but kept herself busy reading and drinking glasses of water, refilling them in the kitchen, and making endless trips to the washroom.

 Atul and her's was an arranged cum love marriage, seven years ago. He had seen her at her cousin's marriage, and a proposal had come through, and everything had worked out perfectly, and she had become his wife at the right age of twenty-four. Now two children later, this. She didn't even want to think about the word. There were absolutely no signs.

The women's magazines have so many articles nowadays that the women reading them must have turned overnight into Sherlock Holmes. I must have slept a little because I dreamt of faceless women going through a mountain of shirts and peering through magnifying glasses.

After doing her MA, she was thinking of doing a computer course along with literary criticism when she got married, and her plans of working part-time were pushed aside when she found out that she was pregnant in the sixth month of her marriage.

She didn't know when sleep took over, but she must not have slept well because when the alarm went off at 5.30 in the morning, she woke up all groggy. The same monotonous school routine was getting to her. The school dabbas were packed, and the children off to school, then she had little time for herself today, and it was good because the moment they all left and she was alone, all she thought about was that little paper she had found.

She couldn't bring herself to make herself a cup of tea as she just flipped through the newspaper to check the movies of the day. Her horoscope read 'Your search for new experience and knowledge takes you further afield now, fresh acquaintances and contacts may even build up to contracts. Ties and bonds of a totally different nature, those that last a lifetime, are also indicated.

Maybe it's all this huge cloud of suspicion. She must ask Atul outright and clear everything up. Then things will get back to normal, or will they? She had been looking forward to Atul's return, but now she wasn't so sure. She got ready as the morning wore on. He would be back by 11:30. She saw herself in the mirror with a critical eye. A ten-kilogram weight gain after her first pregnancy hadn't just melted away as it had for some of her friends. It stayed with her like a devoted friend. Her round face with a clear wheatish complexion and her eyes, which were her best features.

The lavender kameez was her favourite and her most lucky one. She needs everything on her side, she thought as she put on her earrings. This was a scene out of the old Hindi movie songs, wife getting reading for her husband, putting on her Bindi and jewellery.

After that, the cooking done, she sat on the sofa just surfing channels on the television, too restless to watch anything. When the doorbell rang, she jumped up. Pushing back her stray strand of hair behind her ear and rearranging her facial muscles for that bright, welcoming smile. The guilt of her thoughts gnawing inside her, she felt nauseated.

Hi Jaan, she said when she saw Atul standing there leaning against the door. She got a sweet, tired, but happy to be home smile and a hug. As she walked behind him she tried shaking off that niggling doubt. A glass of water, a bath—and then they sat down to a nice lunch and a quiet chat. They spoke of mundane things: pending bills, missed calls, messages, and his travel stories.

"The food was horrid," Atul was saying. "Nothing like homemade dal and rice."

"Are you all right?" Atul asked. Minal jumped with a start—she had been completely lost in her thoughts."Yes, why do you ask?" She asked.

"You seem a little preoccupied," Atul said, putting up his feet on the coffee table and switching on the television.

"Anything the matter?" he asked, already engrossed in the news channel.

Now is the time, Minal thought, but couldn't bring herself to ask him.

"Just tired," she said. "I'll just have a short nap." She got up, avoiding any further conversation, and retired to their bedroom.

But all she did was toss and turn, and finally got up to open the cupboard and get that paper. The paper lay curled in the palm of her hands, and she couldn't bring herself to read it.

Finally hearing the noises within, Atul switched off the television and sauntered in.

"Why aren't you sleeping ?" he asked her," waiting for me." he gave her one of his melting smiles and joined her on the bed.

"When will the kids be back?" Atul asked her with that mischievous twinkle in his eyes.

Minal's heart was torn in two, but love won, and she went into his arms with tears in her eyes.

"What's this?" he asked her, gently turning her face as he wiped her tears, "Miss me that much in four days?" he said, a worried frown gathering on his forehead as she wouldn't stop crying.

Silently, she uncurled her hand and showed him the piece of paper. He took it and read quietly, and said nothing for a few seconds. Finally, with a sigh of resignation, he sat up cross-legged. Minal had second thoughts about that paper, looking at his expression. Suppose she had burnt it and not said a word, she wouldn't have to hear all that Atul was going to say. Her heart beat so rapidly, and a gnawing ache settled in the pit of her stomach as she waited all the while wanting to close her ears.

"I didn't want to tell you this," he was saying.

"Please don't," Minal almost shouted, but no words emerged from her dry mouth.

"Last month when we were visiting my brother Anil's house," he went on.

Where is all this leading to, she wondered impatiently, but decided to hear him through.

"Anil's mobile message had pinged that afternoon and I just glanced at it and saw a message peep into the notification with lots of red hearts and kisses. I had smiled thinking the couple was lucky to be still in love, but the name popped up was not Anita." he paused looking straight at her.

"Then who?" Minal asked apprehensively.

"Suvarna," he said, "someone called Suvarna."

"What!" I exclaimed.

I had found this chit in his shirt's pocket, the one he had lent me for the party.

The next day, I followed Anil and saw him meet this woman holding hands as they walked along the crowded streets, window shopping and laughing. I tried talking to Anil about it. He evaded my questions at first, but after admitting that I had seen them that day, he told me everything. How he had known the girl before marriage, but due to his parents' objections to their relationship, because of it being an intercaste one, they each had married someone else.

No one was getting hurt; they each had their family and children, and they would continue with their lives, he had said.

"Anyways, Bhai sahib, outside things must be kept outside only, not brought home," he tried to control," he said sheepishly, "Sorry you kind of got mixed up in this, please don't tell anyone else he had pleaded with me." I had scolded him, explaining to him the wrong path he was on.

A part of me was so happy as I went into his arms, but now this thing had put that small seed of suspicion in my life. A message beep sounded on Arun's cell, and he turned to switch it off quickly. Why the rush, Minal thought to herself, was it really Anil's story or...

****

10. Full Circle

"Ranjana chai lao,"(Ranjana bring tea) said Mrs Rana, trying to stifle her yawn, "Get some biscuits too." It was nine in the morning and Mrs Rana had a hard time trying to stay awake.

There had been a party at Mrs Johar's place last night, and she had managed to get into bed in the wee hours of the morning. Mrs Rana had a splitting headache and was in no mood to walk up to the medicine cabinet. Her husband, Manoj, as usual, was away on a business tour and wouldn't be back for another week. The children had already left for college.

Mrs. Johar was the wife of her husband's most important business client, and she *had* to attend this party. She hated late nights, all the parties, and people like the Johars.

She had begun to detest the false smiles, the *yes, ma'am*, and all the buttering up. She hadn't eaten anything yesterday and had nursed a single glass of wine until the end.

These headaches had become so frequent lately, they felt as if they had a life of their own.

In her late forties, Mrs Rana had a well-maintained figure thanks to her personal instructor, Sunny, a dusky complexion, and no single good feature to speak of. Mrs Rana was no beauty, and she knew it.

"Bai, chai," Ranjana said, placing the tray with tea on the side table.

Mrs. Rana opened her eyes and sat up gingerly, holding her head. She noticed the aspirin tablet beside a glass of water and gave Ranjana a grateful look. Even her maid had started anticipating her needs.

Had her life become so predictable?

"What would I do without you, Ranju?" Mrs. Rana murmured, rubbing her temples.

Ah heaven! Thought Mrs Rana as she sipped the adrak (ginger) tea. She loved this tea. It reminded her of her past when everything was so simple. Where had that life gone?

It felt like ages since the family had sat down to dinner together; for that matter, it had been a long time since they had even shared the same room. She no longer knew what was happening in her children's lives—who their friends were, what they did, or what they liked.

She and her husband hadn't had a proper conversation in weeks. Their exchanges had been reduced to: *"Hi, how was your day?"* and *"We've got to attend so-and-so's party/reception."*

Manju (Mrs Rana) had been born in a middle-class household in a small sleepy town where nothing ever happened. She had so badly wanted to get out of that place that she had accepted the first proposal that came along from a boy working in Mumbai.

This was her ticket to freedom and bigger things in life. She was lucky that the boy from Mumbai, Manoj, was a good husband and very determined to climb the social ladder of success. In the early days, when they lived in their two-room rented house, she was often snubbed by the neighbours as a country bumpkin. But Manju was determined to climb her own ladder of fashion and style.

The very first step had been moving to a different locality and enrolling in a grooming class, and changing her name to Manasi as soon as they got hold of a little money. Then started the mission of making it big.

She had nagged her quiet, contented husband to quit his low-profile, low-paying job and start his own business. With a bit of luck and a lot of hard work, the business took off. In the end, they had made it— a bungalow, branded clothes, cars, and the best international schools for their children.

It was, on the surface, a fairytale story—rags to riches. But was it really?

Manoj often regaled people at parties with this version of their journey. Manasi had never liked it.

They were totally lost in the high-profile party circuit. In the beginning, it was bliss. Then the boredom set in. Her conscience nudged her gently. All wasn't right, it told her from time to time.

An hour later, her headache had disappeared, and her thoughts were so clear now. That was when she took the most important decision of her life.

The following week, she cancelled all her meetings, declined a party invitation, and worked like she had never before. There was a new spring in her step. The night following her husband's return from his business tour, Manasi broached the subject of a family holiday, and after much persuasion, she managed to convince Manoj to take a weekend break. That done, she set about tackling her children as they returned from a late-night party. Here, a much sterner approach was needed; a threat of cancellation of credit cards did the trick. Rohan and Aditi were stunned to see this new mom.

Everyone put Manasi's behaviour down to menopause. The destination had been kept a secret, and there was a sense of apprehension as, instead of heading toward the airport, they found themselves on a dirt track shortly after leaving the city that evening.

About two hours later, they finally came to a stop.

"Where are we?" they all cried in unison, stiff and irritated from the journey.

They got out to see nothing for miles, just two or three small houses nearby. A few stumbles later, they reached the door of a house.

"Ma, where is the hotel?" Rohan asked in a complaining voice, "I am really tired, no house calls, no relatives, please," he said as he walked reluctantly to the door.

Manasi unlocked the door and stepped in. They were stunned to see rows of candles lit up and a few lanterns hanging in the verandah and inner rooms.

"Wow," everyone said in unison.

"This is so romantic, Mom, are you sure it isn't your anniversary? Then we will be in your way surely," Aditi said teasingly.

Manoj smiled and gave her a questioning look, waiting for an explanation.

"Welcome to our new weekend home," Manasi said in a subdued tone.

There was a pin-drop silence.

"Hungry anyone?" she asked, entering the kitchen. Everyone followed her, their growling stomachs ruling out any doubts.

She had brought along tiffins and everyone ate the simple home-cooked meal sitting at the cosy dining table for the first time in many years. It was heartening to watch them, and Manasi felt tears welling in her eyes.

"Wow, that was great," the children said appreciatively.

"Haven't eaten food like that in the past fifteen years," Manoj added, licking his fingers.

Manasi blushed and said, "I cooked it this afternoon ."

"You mom ?" said Aditi in surprise.

"You can cook, Ma?" Rohan said, eating the roti-sabzi with gusto, his mouth full.

After dinner, they sat outside in the screened verandah. Rohan and Aditi lounged in the hammocks, while Manoj and she sat in the rocking chairs.

No one said a word. The cool breeze drifted through, and in the distance, they could hear the sound of the waves.

"Mom, is that the sea I hear?" Rohan asked.

"Yes," Manasi said, "It's just behind us, we will go there first thing tomorrow morning."

"By the way, where are we ?"Aditi asked.

"Yes, Manju, where are we, and what made you do this?" Manoj asked unknowingly, slipping back to her old name and looking right into her eyes.

She told them everything, all her feelings, her fears for herself and her family, and the rift between them all, and how she had looked for this perfect place and spent her savings buying it.

"You were saving for that precious pearl necklace, na Manju?" Manoj asked.

"You're the most precious pearls in my life, Manoj," Manju said quietly.

She believed her investment would bring in a lot of profit—just watching her family eat and sit together like this felt like one already.

The house was far away from civilization, with no television and no internet. Load shedding was frequent in the area, and electricity was used only for the bare essentials.

Nobody said anything for a while after she finished speaking. Manoj just reached out and held her hand, his eyes filled with tears.

It had been so easy to avoid seeing each other with all the distractions and their busy schedules.

It had become so difficult to even hear each other or have a conversation, with the music blaring and the television constantly tuned to the Sensex.

So very easy to hide behind gadgets, newspapers, parties, and meetings.

The sound of crickets filled the silence. The stars shone brightly, and the moon cast a cool, peaceful light over everything.

"You're right, Ma—we hardly ever spent time together at home," Rohan said.

"We must do this more often," Aditi said quietly.

Manoj was the last one to say, "Thanks to your mother, we have found each other again, let's not lose this ever again."

The kids gave Manoj and Manju a tight hug before turning in for the night.

"My Manju is back again, I've missed her these past years," said Manoj.

"I have missed you too," Manju said, snuggling closer to Manoj.

****

11. An Indian Summer

She swerved inward automatically, avoiding the muddy path—it was a trap for her spike-heeled shoes. *Damn!* This was supposed to be summer, for God's sake, but India's May showers were nothing if not unpredictable.

It was past midnight. With no moon or electricity, and to add to it, the rain pelting down her face, Crystal Claydon could barely keep her eyes open.

She longed for a hot bath and hoped the resort had electricity. Muttering a few choice words about her own stupidity of refusing the ride back to the resort in a friend's car, she pushed back her dripping cinnamon – brown hair that had clung to her equally wet forehead. The distance of one mile had seemed nothing to her, and she had been eager to walk back, taking in the smell and sight of India at nightime.

The informal party had been arranged by the local photographer, Ashok Kurruvilla, at his traditional South Indian home called a 'Tharawad'

A large drop of rainwater hit Crystal directly in her eye, causing her to lose her balance, and slip, falling headlong into a ditch filled with muddy water.

Walking barefoot all the way, stumbling and resembling a drowned rat, she arrived at the gates of the 'Coconut Bay Resort'. The doorman gave her a startled look, but by now she was beyond any care and dragged herself up to the reception desk through the almost deserted lobby, leaving behind puddles of water along the way. The man at the reception hid his emotions quickly and managed a goodnight after a polite inquiry about her health.

Rushing into the elevator, she collided with someone, and a strong pair of arms saved her from another disaster. She raised her head to apologise as she tried to extricate herself from the stranger's arms, when her eyes widened in shock as she recognised her saviour.

"You don't seem to have changed much, still very eager to get into my arms", he said mockingly, taking his own sweet time in letting her go.

Crystal was too dazed to speak. Hari, her husband, still had this effect on her. Her pounding heart was enough evidence. She felt herself drown in his deep brown eyes, and all five long years just seemed to melt away. At six feet four inches, he towered over her—and even in her heels, she still felt small standing before him.

Her mind went back to the past, the first time she met him at the county hospital in England, in fact, collided with him would be the right thing to say. Her dad had been admitted for a bypass, and she was deeply distraught. Hari, the resident doctor, was just on his way out after a nerve-wracking thirty-six hours of emergency duty.

"Hello? Cat got your tongue? You never seemed to have any trouble finding words."

Now he was openly laughing at her.

"What are you doing here in India?"

Keeping a tight hold on her volatile temper was becoming increasingly difficult—with her face covered in mud and her flimsy dress clinging to her body. She could feel his burning gaze and looked up to find him lingering on her curves in an all-too-familiar way.

"You've changed. You look different. These past years have filled you out," he said.

"You seemed to have no time to listen to my words anyway," she managed to reply coolly. "I'm here on an assignment to write a travel-related article on Kerala."

"What about you?" she asked him.

"I am here for an international conference on tuberculosis," he answered, looking searchingly into her eyes when a look of concern passed across his face.

"You've hurt yourself. There's a small gash on your forehead," he said, examining the wound gently.

"Let's go to my room," he added, sensing her reluctance.

"It could get infected, just needs some cleaning," he added mockingly, "I promise not to eat you up."

She knew she shouldn't be allowing this—a small voice in her head warned her.

But dear God, it felt so good to be this close to him again. When his hand accidentally touched her, she felt him stiffen.

Five years back, they were married within three weeks of knowing each other. It had seemed like a fairytale at that time; she had met her prince, but it took only a year for it to end. His busy routine kept them apart, and she got bored with her solitary life at their apartment until the day she found out she was pregnant. She was ecstatic about the news, but Hari wasn't—burdened by his meagre salary and long, exhausting hours.

They had their first real argument, and she had rushed out… never to return.

She had refused to answer his calls and sent him a message about her miscarriage. She waited for the divorce papers, which never came.

Crystal had run away to her aunt's place in the country to lick her wounds. She had picked up the pieces of her life and never looked back, only to come face to face with it again.

"Too long," he muttered.

"And five endless years…" Hari sighed—a harsh sound of capitulation. "I went crazy searching for you. Oh God, Crystal…"

He pulled her into his arms.

To feel safe—secure—in his arms, even though there was no future. Reality would return, and she would face it then.

She turned her head and buried her face in the curve of his neck, feeling the strong pulse throb against her lips.

All the unanswered questions, all the doubts, just seemed to fade away.

Nothing else mattered anymore.

There is something I have to tell you, she said, and led him to the hotel lobby.

"Mummy," a small, energetic bundle rushed up to her, and she scooped up her son into her arms

Hari watched him and Crystal with stunned eyes, a questioning look on them. Crystal silently nodded, afraid this would change everything.

But strong hands engulfed them both.

Hari's hands framed her face tenderly. "I've never stopped loving you," he said.

Until they both had to let down the squirming child who looked up to Hari, perplexed, an exact copy of him, down to his curly black hair.

****

12. An Exchange

He was the second in a line of students who had come to stay with us.

"Patrick," he had said as soon as he entered our home, introducing himself and shaking my hand all at once. "I'm sweating like a pig," he added, despite it being his fourth bath of the day.

"I think I'll sleep now, Aai. See you at dinner."

The students were encouraged to address everyone as family members—we were his extended family for those three weeks.

It was breakfast when he finally got up. Thankfully, I had managed to feed him a three-egg omelette before he slept, knowing this would happen. I had gotten the guestroom all ready for the requirements of the exchange association.

A computer with internet, an attached bathroom, a writing table, and a cupboard. It had taken us two weeks to drag all the furniture around and empty the closet. My teenage son and younger daughter were very excited about this.

The last one was a girl from Brazil. She adapted quickly— eating with her hands and eagerly learning how to make chapattis.

"I love your flatbreads," she'd say, and by the time she left, she had become quite the expert. Our maid cried the most when she left—and missed her the most too, for obvious reasons.

My son had visited Brazil last year and had the most amazing time with her family.

It was eleven in the morning when Patrick finally made an appearance at the breakfast table. The tall, blonde, blue-eyed eighteen-year-old looked a little disoriented at first, but seemed fine after a hearty breakfast of aloo paratha and curds.

I chalked it up to jet lag and hypoglycemia as he slowly got back to normal, sipping his coffee.

"It's so peaceful here at home," he said, listening to the birds chirping in the garden. With everyone off to work and college, it really was.

Just then, a vendor hollered, and Patrick's stunned expression was almost comical. Within seconds, he had set his coffee mug down on the table and rushed outside.

I ran out too, trying to stop him from stepping onto the road—my face mirroring his bewilderment at what had suddenly gotten into him.

He was standing outside the gate, watching the *raddiwala*—the Indian recyclist who collects old newspapers, furniture, and other discarded items from each household.

"Pay po…wa…r," Patrick said in an almost perfect imitation and grinned at us. Kamala bai and I were just standing there with our mouths open. I had not expected that, but looking at the pure joy on his face, I ended up laughing, not before I had appeased the vendor, telling him the boy was new and did not know our ways.

"You shouldn't rush out of the house imitating people—you never know, they might take offense," I explained to Patrick. There were so many things I had to tell him.

That afternoon, Patrick lazed on the sofa in the hall, flipping through television channels until the children and my husband, Shekhar, returned from work.

He was fascinated by the programmes—the Hindi movies, the songs—and he had so many questions. The news horrified him, and by the end of it all, we were both exhausted. After a light lunch of salad and chutney sandwiches, we took a nap in the afternoon.

Tea time, everyone had gathered around the table. Patrick had asked the children everything about school, colleges. Aditi and Manav asked him a lot of questions about Germany and his schooling, and life there.

After dinner, Shekhar asked Patrick what he wanted to do the next day, it was a Sunday and his holiday.

"Baba, I just want to take a ride around the city—see the traffic, the market area, Aditi and Manav's college and school in the morning. Nothing particular; just want to chill. Next week is our big Delhi–Agra trip," Patrick said, sitting cross-legged on the sofa.

"Ok," Baba agreed quickly, it was a simple request and a holiday was a holiday, he thought. A hearty lunch, an afternoon nap and maybe dinner out."

Everyone seemed to agree.

"Baba, I want to sit on a two-wheeler, the rickshaw, and of course the local bus," Patrick said excitedly, counting each one on his fingers.

"We can include that bike ride when we go to the market for shopping tomorrow morning and the day after, Aai, and you can sit in the 'Pune Darshan' bus, it's just like the local bus, just colourful, and see all the heritage sights in Pune."

After a hearty breakfast of 'Idli Sambar' the next morning, Shekhar searched for another helmet for Patrick, as they both set off on the kinetic after Shekhar had given him some instructions.

"Yoohoo!" Patrick spread his arms wide as soon as Shekhar set off—but he quickly dropped them, probably after being duly admonished.

They returned after two hours. Shekhar was smiling but looked exhausted, while Patrick was full of energy, pretending to lift weights and talking nonstop—recounting everything he had seen in the market. His face was red from the heat.

"Just wait, Patrick! Why didn't you take the hat I left on the chair?" I scolded him, handing them both a tall glass of freshly squeezed lime juice.

"All you moms are the same," Patrick smiled, gulping down the juice all in one go. "What is that taste ?"

"It's 'Pudina' (mint leaves)," I said, taking his glass.

"You know, Aai, there were such colourful vegetables and such a huge mound of green and red chillies, I was sneezing and sneezing every time we passed them!" Patrick recounted everything he had experienced, and I found myself envying his excitement. I also realized how truly observant he was.

"I want to wear a turban, Aai! It's so colourful—and that '*topi*!' The people were shouting louder than their neighbours, all trying to attract customers. The smells and colours were everywhere! And the traffic—so many people!"

He was so excited he could hardly sit still.

They discussed each other's lives in their countries. Shekhar asked him about his dad's work and his daily routine. They were so engrossed in chatting and didn't realise it was time for lunch until Aai called them in, and they made their way to the dining table.

"Wow! This is like a Christmas spread," Patrick exclaimed, seeing all the dishes.

I had put aside the preparation for Patrick before adding the masalas and had made lots of salad and kept some 'mithais'(sweets) just in case.

"You have spoons and forks!" he exclaimed and gave their daughter Aditi an accusing look. Everyone looked at Patrick for an explanation.

"When Aditi had visited us, she told us that Indians eat with their hands and there were no forks and spoons here, so I have brought some plastic ones from home, even collecting the ones on the airline."

All of us burst out laughing—and so did Patrick—when he looked at Aditi, who couldn't stop giggling.

"Your food isn't spicy at all. I thought Indian food was?" Patrick commented as he put another spoonful of 'Dal' in his mouth.

"Here, taste mine Aditi said, giving him a spoonful of hers before anyone could stop her.

"Oh my God!" he exclaimed, the smile wiped clean off his face as he reached for his glass of water—coughing, with tears running down his cheeks, his face turning bright red.

"Aditi, why did you do that?" I scolded her, but she had already given him a 'Gulab jamun', a 'sweet syrupy ball' to eat, which Patrick ate only after he had looked at me for assurance.

"That was a spoon of fire, how can you eat that so calmly?" Patrick looked at them all with a new respect.

I had kept your food aside before adding the spices, Patrick," I said, "We are used to this right from childhood. Our taste buds have developed accordingly. What do you have at home for lunch and dinner?"

"Your taste buds must be burned out by now for sure," Patrick said, nodding his head while taking another bite of the Gulab jamun. "This thing just saved my life ."

"We have bread, potatoes, meat, cabbage, salad, rice and peas with very little spice and not yellow in colour. How come everything is colourful here? What is that yellow coloured stuff?" He asked.

"It's turmeric," Shekhar said. "It's a powder made from a dried root. It has medicinal and antibacterial properties."

Patrick even had a go at eating with both hands, tearing the chapatti like a piece of paper—until Manav showed him the right way.

"Use your right hand, not your left," he told him, anticipating the question and promising to explain later.

After lunch, everyone went into their own rooms. It was like an unspoken decision after that heavy meal.

Everyone had a good two-hour nap and came out all sleepy-eyed to have their tea.

When I offered Patrick some biscuits, he shook his head, "No, Mom, I cannot fit a single thing in my tummy now. It will surely burst!"

Each one came out after their nap and sat in front of the television with a dazed expression.

I was wondering if anyone would agree to the dinner plan, or if I would have to make 'kadhi khichdi'.

After tea every one decided to climb the 'Laxman tekdi' behind their house. It was a hillock with a small mandir on top. The exercise refreshed them, and when they came back an hour later, everyone got into their rooms to get dressed, and Shekhar asked me to get ready.

They decided to visit the newly opened French restaurant in the Regent Park area. After placing their orders, the soft music lulled everyone into a calm silence as they took in the elegant atmosphere.

After we had polished off the dessert and paid the bill, we decided to go for a long drive to Panchami Lake.

Everyone agreed the food was good—until Patrick said, quite frankly, "The French food in India tastes Indian." We all burst out laughing.

Patrick was excited to get on the bus! Aai, though not as thrilled—having seen these places many times—was still happy to have a day off from cooking and was looking forward to shopping at the Khadi Centre near Aga Khan Palace.

Shaniwar Wada, the historic seat of the Peshwas in Pune, had the busiest and oldest market around. The *darshan* of the famous Dagadu Sheth Ganpati and Saras Baug

Ganpati, she told Patrick, was an auspicious beginning to his visit to India.

Patrick had a thousand questions about the elephant god!

The next day, I took him to meet some of our relatives, introducing him to both first and second cousins. That weekend, there was a wedding—my first cousin's eldest daughter, Swati. Patrick was in for a concentrated dose of Indian culture.

Her cousin Moushmi, a bored housewife always on the lookout for excitement, treated Patrick's visit like a festival. Out came the jari silk sari, steaming ginger tea, hot samosas—and an endless stream of questions. She had even invited a few neighbours to join in.

Patrick was clearly enjoying himself, basking in the attention. But after about an hour, I noticed him trying to stifle a yawn, slowly sinking into the sofa, his energy starting to fade.

Moushmi's daughter, Swati, walked in at just the right moment, her arms full of shopping bags. After the introductions were made, the two of them quickly struck up a conversation.

"So, is yours a love marriage or an arranged one?" Patrick asked.

"An arranged one," Swati replied, almost apologetically. "Our parents met, decided, matched our horoscopes, showed me his photograph… and we met twice—six months ago."

"Are you allowed to meet before marriage?" Patrick was probably seeing a person having an arranged marriage for the very first time.

Sensing Swati's unease, Moushmi stepped in and handed Patrick a stack of old photo albums to browse through.

Inside were sepia-toned photographs of our grandparents in traditional attire, village scenes, and memories from another era—enough to keep him occupied for a good hour.

When I finally got up to leave, Patrick shot me a grateful glance.

The days leading up to the wedding were a blur of *sangeet, mehendi,* and the *haldi* ceremony. Patrick had all his wishes fulfilled.

I'd bought him a salwar kurta and a readymade dhoti, along with a *topi*—and on the wedding day, he even got to wear a turban.

Getting him ready, though, was another story. Shekhar had to help with everything—from pricking his finger while stitching something, to struggling with a stubborn knot in the waistband. In the end, I gave up and replaced it with an elastic one.

Patrick was having a great time—asking the meaning of every *vidhi* (some of which even I couldn't explain), and taking videos and photos of everything... including the Indian loo!

He'd even prepared a group dance for the *sangeet* ceremony, and to everyone's surprise, not only danced but sang the song quite well too.

Then Patrick left for the Golden Triangle.

Aarti finally had some time on her hands—to catch up on all her neglected chores and take a breather from her many roles: cook, guide, babysitter, interpreter.

But she missed Patrick. She had grown to love him like her own, and found herself buying three of everything each time she went out.

The week flew by, and soon Aarti was back at the station, waiting to pick him up.

Patrick's face lit up the moment he saw her, and he gave her a tight hug. He looked exhausted and a little pale, but still managed to offer her a tired smile.

So Aarti too decided to keep quiet, and the journey ended in comfortable silence.

"I have the Delhi belly," he announced as soon as we reached home, making a dash for the bathroom.

So *that* had been the reason for his pale look, Aarti thought to herself, as she called the family doctor and took him to the clinic that very evening.

By the next evening, he was feeling much better—the medicines, along with plenty of fluids and juice, had clearly helped. That night, he joined us for a simple meal of moong dal khichdi and curds.

"You know what?" he began excitedly, before any of us could ask what all he'd seen. "A man tried to sell me a pig."

"What?!" I exclaimed.

"I was almost tempted to buy him and bring him home for you, Mom," he said teasingly. "But the pig was so dirty—and then I thought about all the work you'd have cleaning him up."

He was grinning now, and Aditi gave him a playful punch.

The next fifteen days passed in a blur of shopping and trying out new restaurants. They even managed a quiet overnight trip to Mulshi Lake—just the five of them. It was peaceful and relaxing.

Afternoons were spent learning and playing games like *Ludo, Snakes and Ladders*, and cards. But Patrick fell in love with *carrom*. He invited anyone and everyone to play, and over time, became quite good at it.

Soon, it was time for Patrick to leave, and a quiet sadness began to settle in. He felt it too, though he tried not to show it. He spoke less, often sitting with a book, maybe slowly switching off—preparing himself to say goodbye.

Sometimes, he'd walk into the kitchen without a word, give me a tight hug, and leave again.

Finally, the day to say goodbye arrived, and Aarti could not hold back her tears. Patrick had tears in his eyes too—especially when she handed him a parting gift: the house keys. A reminder that he always had a home and family in India, and could return anytime.

We had also bought him a carrom board and promised to ship it to him. But Patrick insisted on taking it along, despite our warnings that it might not be allowed. As expected, it wasn't—and we ended up bringing it back home with us.

A few months passed. The emails started becoming less frequent. The only lingering reminder of Patrick is the carrom board, still packed and leaning quietly against the wall, waiting to be taken to the post office.

Somehow, every time I look at it, the exchange feels incomplete.

Tomorrow, I'll send it, I tell myself.

****

13. Scorpion

"Mele kaay kelas hey!" she screamed loudly.

Oh God in heaven—that really hurt.

Saap-saap! The sound of those thin wooden sticks cutting through the air was sharp and terrifying. Then came the burning pain—like red-hot needles searing into my skin. I shut my eyes tight and stamped my feet. As if that would help. I didn't even use them to run away—just hopped about in that tiny space as Aaji [Grandmother] kept on with the beating.

There was nowhere to run. On one side, the iron cot railings. On the other, a damp wall. I was trapped in a space no more than two feet wide.

The green distemper was peeling off the wall. And all I could think of during the punishment was: *Gosh, my new frock is getting all that green stuff on it.*

It was all over after six *saaps*—a matter of a few seconds, and not even a tell-tale mark on the backs of my legs.

Aaji must have worked in some torture department before *Ajoba* married her, I fumed, and ran away to sulk under the coconut tree.

She was really mad this time. I had spat on her—and even hit her on the head with the clothes-drying stick. She had cried out in pain, unaware of my evil intentions. Her back was turned towards me, as she sat on her haunches at the sunken, old-fashioned wash basin in the kitchen, scrubbing the dirty lunch dishes. The blow was the last thing she expected.

I hated that cooped-up place. I hated her. I hated everyone in the world at that moment.

I wasn't going to apologize—and that was that. My five-year-old stubborn brain refused to accept defeat. This was the real thing. *This was war.*

I wiped my nose on the back of my hand and cursed my grandmother again. Sitting in the cool breeze, my imagination took off. Aaji was now the witch. I was Gretel from the Hansel and Gretel story. She must be starting the fire under the cauldron, waiting to cook me in it.

Suddenly, a gust of strong wind blew, and the coconut tree swayed above me.

Aaji came running out, crying, "You'll be the death of one of us! How many times have I told you not to sit under that tree? Those coconuts will fall on your head!"

She hugged me close, wiping her tears—and mine—with the soft cotton *pallu* of her sari. My thin arms clutched tightly around her waist, and somehow she managed to carry us both into the house.

The war was over in a minute.

"Aaji, I'm hungry," Rani said—and was promptly handed a *besan laddoo*, which Aaji had brought with her in anticipation.

We walked back into the house, hand in hand.

Grandma Parvati was my maternal grandmother. Since my mom worked in an office, I stayed with Aaji until she returned at seven in the evening. In her fifties, Aaji looked younger than her age, with her jet-black hair tied up in a ribbon—though, with due respect, the dye stick barely touched her shoulders. Always bustling around in her plump figure, she had an energy that belied her age.

"Don't call me Aaji, call me 'Mothi Aai'—'Elder Mother'. You see, I'm not that old," she would insist.

With no idiot box (television) at home, there wasn't much to do. I would watch my grandmother work. It was just the two of us during the day, as Grandpa left early for his job as a clerk at a paint factory on the outskirts of the village.

The farm had long stopped yielding good crops, and now weeds had completely taken over. One day, Rani sat watching Mothi Aai with fascination as she sat at her old dressing table, applying 'kumkum' (red sindoor) on her forehead.

This was a whole ritual in itself. First, she dabbed a bit of oil on her forehead. Then, she held up a piece of paper with a diamond-shaped cut-out in the centre and gently applied a pinch of the kumkum powder over it. She slowly lifted the paper—voila, a perfect red dot, like a work of art.

Her eyes met Rani's in the mirror, and they both smiled.

"Aaji—sorry, Mothi Aai—why don't you just buy those stick-on bindis?" Rani asked.

Resting her hands on Rani's shoulders, Mothi Aai smiled. "Then you wouldn't be sitting here every evening watching me like you do now. Besides, those stick-on ones are no fun."

"Come on, Rani, let's get ready. Your Granddad will be home any minute—it's nearly 5:30 p.m.," she said, quickly straightening her saree and slipping on her chappals.

"Mothi Aai, may I have just one more salted raw mango piece?" Rani asked.

"They've been cut for the pickles, Rani. You've already eaten way too many." But seeing Rani's crestfallen face, she relented, "Okay, just one."

By the time Grandpa arrived, Rani had managed to sneak in four or five pieces. She ran toward him and shouted, "Hi Nana!" and he swung her high into the air.

"How is my Rani beta today?" he asked.

"I got the usual dose of punishment today," she replied, launching into the full story.

"You shouldn't do that, beta," Grandpa gently scolded her. "What if you had hurt her really badly?"

After some refreshments and a bit more chit-chat, it was time to begin dinner preparations. They all followed Grandpa inside. Grandma put the rice cooker on the stove, cut some vegetables, and then headed to the bedroom for one of her strange rituals.

"Why do you do this?" Rani asked, leaning against the doorframe, watching her in fascination.

"This keeps my brain fresh and my hair black," Grandma replied.

She was upside down—legs tied together and resting against the wooden cupboard.

About five minutes later, Grandpa peeked in, then suddenly strode across the room, grabbed her legs, and gently lifted her up and set her aside.

It happened so quickly.

"Hey! What's wrong with you? Why did you do that?" Grandma said indignantly.

Grandpa pointed silently toward the cupboard. "Just look there."

We all turned to look—and what a shocking sight. A huge, horrible black scorpion lay exactly where Grandma had just been resting her head.

We were too stunned to scream. I jumped onto the nearest side table. Grandma sat there on the floor, mouth wide open, legs still tied, staring at the scorpion while Grandpa took care of it.

****